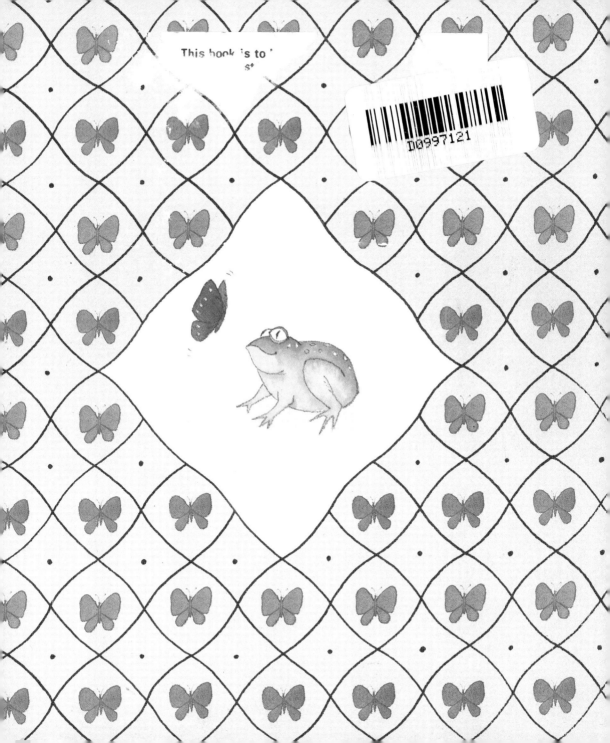

This book is to
st

For Edward, Clare
and Alexander

Copyright © Zita Newcome 1991
All rights reserved
First published in Great Britain 1991
by Julia MacRae
an imprint of the Random Century Group
20 Vauxhall Bridge Road, London SW1V 2SA

Printed in Hong Kong

British Library Cataloguing in Publication Data
Newcome, Zita
Rosie goes exploring
I. Title
823'.914 [J]

ISBN 1-85681-170-0

Rosie Goes Exploring

Zita Newcome

Julia MacRae Books

LONDON SYDNEY AUCKLAND JOHANNESBURG

Rosie has found her grandpa's old hat in the attic.

She goes outside to explore his garden. It is like a jungle.

Rosie finds a pool where goldfish swim round and round.

She watches a cat slink by
in the tall grass

. . . and finds a squashy caterpillar on a cabbage.

In the greenhouse,
Rosie eats a tomato,

and when she sets off again,
she sees a shaggy dog sleeping
in the bushes.

Then Rosie plays on a swing,

and gathers some flowers from
a grassy bank.

In an old shed she finds a frog

hiding in the dark.

Rosie climbs up into a tree-house
and watches the birds.

And then it is time to go indoors.

"Hello, Rosie. Have you been exploring?" asks Grandpa.

"Yes," says Rosie.